The Fourth Floor Twins and the
Sand Castle Contest

The
Fourth Floor TwinS
and the
Sand Castle Contest

DAVID A. ADLER
Illustrated by Irene Trivas

Viking Kestrel

VIKING KESTREL
Published by the Penguin Group
Viking Penguin Inc., 40 West 23rd Street, New York, New York 10010, U.S.A.
Penguin Books Ltd, 27 Wrights Lane, London W8 5TZ, England
Penguin Books Australia Ltd, Ringwood, Victoria, Australia
Penguin Books Canada Ltd, 2801 John Street, Markham, Ontario, Canada L3R 1B4
Penguin Books (N.Z.) Ltd, 182-190 Wairau Road, Auckland 10, New Zealand

Penguin Books Ltd, Registered Offices: Harmondsworth, Middlesex, England

First published in 1988 by Viking Penguin Inc.
Published simultaneously in Canada
1 3 5 7 9 10 8 6 4 2
Text copyright © David A. Adler, 1988
Illustrations copyright © Irene Trivas, 1988
All rights reserved

Library of Congress Cataloging in Publication Data
Adler, David A.
The fourth floor twins and the sand castle contest/by David A. Adler;
illustrated by Irene Trivas. p. cm.
Summary: In an extraordinary day at the beach, after winning a sand castle contest,
two sets of twins resolve the mystery of the disappearance of a rich woman's dog.
ISBN 0-670-82150-0 [1. Mystery and detective stories. 2. Twins—Fiction.]
I. Trivas, Irene, ill. II. Title. PZ7.A2615Fog 1988 [Fic]—dc19 88-10831 CIP

Printed in the United States of America by Haddon Craftsmen, Bloomsburg, Pennsylvania
Set in Times Roman

To Esther Hautzig

The Fourth Floor Twins and the
Sand Castle Contest

CHAPTER ONE

"Soda. Ice-cold soda here!" a man on the beach called out. "Ice cream, ice-cold ice cream!"

"We'll make a hippo poking its head out of the water," Gary Young said, as he walked onto the beach. Gary's twin brother, Kevin, and their friends, twin sisters Donna and Diane Shelton, were with him.

The beach was crowded. Some people had come to swim and sit in the sunshine. Many others had come for the *Morning News* Festival and the sand castle contest.

"Martin, are you there?" a woman walking ahead of the twins asked. She was wearing a bright green bathing suit. She was carrying a folding beach chair, a beach umbrella, a large straw bag, and a blanket. A small boy held onto a corner of the blanket. He was carrying an open box of animal crackers.

"Yes, I'm here," the boy answered.

"What? I don't hear you. Where are you?"

The woman dropped her beach chair. She turned and looked for her son, but she still didn't see him.

"He's right here, behind the umbrella," Diane told the woman.

"Humph," the woman said, as she picked up the beach chair. "Martin, when I call, I want you to answer me."

Donna and Diane smiled when they heard that. Before they left for the beach, their

2

mother had said the same thing to Diane. Diane speaks very softly and sometimes her mother doesn't hear her.

The twins are all ten years old and are in the fifth grade. Some people call them the Fourth Floor Twins because the Youngs and the Sheltons live on the fourth floor of the same apartment building.

The twins walked past a large snack stand selling french fries, soda, ice cream, milkshakes, and hamburgers. Nearby was a smaller stand selling suntan oils, beach hats, sand toys, newspapers, and magazines.

"Martin. Martin, are you there?" the woman asked.

"Yes, here I am," the small boy shouted.

"Look, that's where we have to go," Gary said. He pointed to a table near the edge of the water. Tacked onto the table was a sign: *MORNING NEWS* SAND CASTLE CON-TEST.

Gary had entered the contest. Diane would

help him. Kevin and Donna came to the beach to watch the contest and to swim.

There was a line of people waiting by the table. Gary and Diane joined the end of the line. Kevin and Donna walked off and looked for a place to put their blanket.

"I'm Betty Lane," the woman behind the table told the man at the head of the line. "I'm the chief judge in the sand castle contest."

Betty Lane asked the man his name. She checked if the man was entered in the contest. Then she told him where to build his sand castle. And she told him that he was allowed to have one helper.

"Don't begin working yet. We're waiting for Mrs. Rogers. She owns the *Morning News*. I'll blow my whistle and tell you when to start."

Gary and Diane heard Betty Lane repeat this to each person waiting in line.

"I'm Betty Lane," she said again when

it was Gary and Diane's turn.

"We know," Gary told her.

Diane leaned forward and said in her soft voice, "We heard you tell all the others about the contest. He's Gary Young and I'm Diane Shelton."

Betty Lane looked at a sheet of paper attached to a clipboard and said, "You will work in section 14."

Near the water were roped-off sections of sand. Gary and Diane found section 14.

Gary turned his beach bag upside down. Two small shovels, a plastic bucket, some sticks, and a water-sprayer fell onto the sand. Diane took the sticks and shovels and lined them up. She wiped the sand from the water-sprayer and placed it in the bucket.

"Look what that woman brought," Gary whispered to Diane. He pointed to the woman in section 13. She was holding a large sheet of paper cut into the shape of a turtle.

"And look at him," Diane said. She pointed to the man in section 12. He held a piece of paper cut into the shape of a car. There were marks on the paper showing him where to put the bumpers, lights, and doors.

Gary and Diane watched people running in and out of the water. They saw lifeguards sitting on high wooden chairs, watching the people swim in the ocean. Gary and Diane saw people lying in the sun and small children playing in the sand. They saw a few people turn to look at the beach entrance. Then others turned.

Diane turned and said, "Look! I think Mrs. Rogers is coming."

CHAPTER TWO

Kevin and Donna had just spread out their blanket. They turned to look, too. They saw two men come through the beach entrance. The men carried long, wide wood boards. The men dropped the boards onto the sand, one after the other. When they had dropped them all, they rushed back to get more. One of the lifeguards moved the boards. The ends of the boards touched and made a wooden walkway on the sand.

At the end of the walkway, the two men placed a few boards together. Then they brought out a large wicker chair and put it on the boards.

"Look, here she comes," Diane said.

A tall woman wearing a long white dress walked onto the beach. She wore gold necklaces and gold bracelets. A large straw hat with a floppy brim was on her head. She held a dog's leash.

A small white dog followed her. There

were jewels on the dog's collar. The woman sat in the chair. She dropped the dog's leash and the dog sat next to her. A man wearing a black uniform and cap stood behind them.

Trill. Trill.

Betty Lane blew a whistle.

"Welcome to our third annual sand castle building contest, sponsored by Mrs. Annette Rogers and the *Morning News.*"

People sunning themselves on blankets and beach towels sat up and listened. A few

people who were swimming in the ocean came out to hear Betty Lane. She spoke slowly and in a loud voice.

"The winners will be given a *Morning News* beach umbrella as a prize. And a picture of them will be on the front page of tomorrow's *Morning News*."

Gary told Diane, "If we win, I'm going to cut our picture out and frame it."

Betty Lane said, "Robert Wool, the famous artist, will be one of the judges."

An old man with white hair hanging to his shoulders stood next to Betty Lane. He waved to the people on the beach.

"Barbara Sands, the hostess of the radio program 'Lunchtime with Barbara,' will also be a judge."

A woman with short brown hair and wearing many necklaces and bracelets stood next to Robert Wool. She waved and her bracelets jangled. She turned and waved to the people standing behind her. Then she put her fingers to her lips, kissed them, and waved some more.

"Thank you, that's enough," Betty Lane said.

"And I am the head judge. My name is Betty Lane. I am the owner of Lane Art Gallery. We are on Fourth Street and are open Monday through Friday."

Gary handed the bucket to Diane. "As soon as she tells us to begin, you get some water."

Betty Lane said, "We call this a sand *castle* contest. But in the next two hours you can build anything you want out of sand."

Trill.

Betty Lane blew her whistle and called out, "You may begin."

Diane ran to the ocean and filled the bucket with water. Gary patted the sand in his section smooth. Then he took a stick and drew an outline of the hippo.

13

People in the other sections were busy, too. They were outlining, digging, and filling buckets with water. The girl in section 9 had brought many buckets to the beach. She ran to the ocean again and again until all the buckets were filled with water.

Kevin and Donna stopped to watch the man in section 6. He was drawing an outline in the sand with a long stick. His wife was standing in the section with him. They argued about which way the sea monster should face.

Arf. Arf.

Mrs. Rogers walked along the wooden path and looked at the people making outlines in the sand. Her small white dog barked as it walked behind her.

The man from section 12 rushed past Kevin and Donna toward the beach entrance. He was carrying an empty bucket.

"Martin," the woman wearing the green bathing suit called as she walked past.

Donna and Kevin watched the girl in section 9 fill a tall plastic cup with wet sand. She turned the cup over to make towers for her sand castle.

"Martin. Martin."

Kevin walked over and watched two boys in section 4 dig sand away from their outline.

"We're making a baseball player," one of the boys told Kevin.

"Martin. Martin."

"He'll be standing with his bat held high, just waiting to hit the ball," the other boy said.

Donna ran to where Kevin was standing. "Martin is not with his mother and he's not on their blanket," Donna told Kevin. "I said we'd help find him. This time Martin is really lost!"

CHAPTER THREE

"Where is she?" Kevin asked.

Donna pointed to the woman in the green bathing suit. She was standing next to a red beach umbrella.

Donna and Kevin ran to her. "Don't worry. We'll find your son," Kevin said.

"We're good at finding people," Donna told the woman.

"Martin is always running off," the woman said. "He's just a small boy."

Arf. Arf.

"He may be watching some of the people in the sand castle contest," Kevin said.

They walked from section to section. A crowd had gathered around the woman in section 2. She had a bucket of very wet sand. She took a handful of wet sand and let it drip. As the drops of wet sand piled up, they formed what looked like the tower of an old castle.

Donna pushed through the crowd and looked for Martin. He wasn't there.

Trill.

A lifeguard blew a whistle. He was standing on the seat of his high wooden chair and waving to swimmers not to go out too deep.

"Oh no!" Martin's mother yelled. She ran to the edge of the water. Kevin and Donna followed her.

"Martin can't swim. He's only four years old," the woman said as she ran along the edge of the water and looked for her son.

Kevin and Donna went into the water. Kevin was careful not to disturb any of the swimmers. But Donna thought only about finding Martin. When she saw a child who looked like Martin, she splashed through the water as she ran to him. Some people scolded Donna and told her not to run. Others quickly got out of her way.

Kevin, Donna, and Martin's mother looked among the swimmers. A few birds flew overhead. Kevin watched the birds fly lower and lower. They landed on an almost empty area of beach. Kevin saw birds fly from other directions and land in the same area. He walked out of the water.

"Where are you going?" Donna asked.

"I just remembered Martin's box of animal crackers."

"What?" Donna asked as she ran to catch up with Kevin.

Kevin and Donna walked away from the water and onto dry sand. They walked far from the *Morning News* Festival. This part of the beach was not crowded. As Kevin and Donna came closer, the birds began to fly off. Then Kevin and Donna saw Martin. He was sitting in the sand and crying.

Kevin ran to Martin. He told Martin that they'd take him to his mother. But the boy didn't stop crying.

"This is why he's crying," Donna said. She held up a box of animal crackers. "It spilled. That's what the birds were eating."

Kevin waited with Martin. Donna went to get his mother.

A short while later, the woman in the green bathing suit ran toward Martin with her hands held out. "Oh, my baby!" she cried.

She picked up her son and hugged him for a long time. Then she put him down and said, "Don't you ever run off again. I was so worried."

The small boy looked at his mother. He smiled. Then she picked him up and hugged him some more.

Kevin and Donna began to walk back toward the *Morning News* Festival.

"Oh, thank you, thank you," the woman called to them.

"You're welcome," Kevin called back.

People at the sand castle contest were

busy. Some were still digging and piling up sand. Others were beginning to shape their sculptures. Small groups of people stood around and watched.

"Look, Gary is shaping the head of the hippo," Kevin said.

Donna said, "I'm looking at Mrs. Rogers. She's sitting just where she was before. But her dog isn't there."

CHAPTER FOUR

Kevin turned to look at Mrs. Rogers. She was sitting on the wicker chair and smiling.

"The man in the black uniform isn't there either," Kevin said. "He probably took the dog for a walk."

Donna looked among the many people watching the sand castle contest. "There he is." Mrs. Rogers's driver was watching the woman who was building a sand castle by dripping wet sand.

"And look here," Donna said. She pointed to smooth areas of sand in the shape of triangles. A trail of them led to where Mrs. Rogers was sitting. Donna turned and looked the other way. She saw that the trail continued across the beach.

Donna said, "When the dog ran off, it dragged its leash. That's what made these marks."

"Let's go tell Mrs. Rogers," Kevin said.

Donna walked ahead. "No," she said. "We have to follow the trail now. If we wait, people will walk across it."

The dog's paw prints were lost in the dry sand. But the smooth marks left by the leash were still there.

Donna ran through the sand as she followed the trail. Kevin followed it more slowly. After a while, he turned and looked to see if the dog had returned to Mrs. Rogers. It hadn't.

The trail led to a large blue blanket. A

man was standing next to it. He had just arrived and was opening a beach umbrella. Two boys were sitting on the blanket. They were emptying a large beach bag.

"Hey, where's the popcorn?" one of the boys asked.

Donna lifted the blanket.

"What are you doing?" the man asked.

"I'm looking for a small white dog."

"There's no dog under the blanket. Just sand," the man said.

"Come on," Kevin told Donna.

Donna followed Kevin around the blue blanket. There they found more smooth areas of sand in the shape of triangles.

Donna walked ahead again. The trail led closer to the water. There, in the wet sand, she and Kevin found paw prints.

Kevin and Donna had walked a long way from the *Morning News* Festival. There were only a few people on the beach here. Kevin and Donna followed the trail back onto dry sand.

They followed the trail to a large, locked wooden shed. The lifeguards kept their suntan lotions, bathing suits, whistles, and other supplies in the shed.

Kevin walked around the shed. But he didn't find any more smooth areas of sand.

The trail had ended.

Then Donna called out, "Look! Look what I found!" She held up a dog's leash.

CHAPTER FIVE

Donna gave Kevin the leash. She looked quickly across the beach. Then she started to walk away.

"Where are you going?" Kevin asked.

"To look for the dog."

"Wait a minute," Kevin said. "Don't run ahead without thinking. Wait. Let's think this whole thing out."

Kevin looked at the leash. He leaned against the shed and thought.

Donna stood next to Kevin. She watched him think for a moment. She leaned against the shed, too. She began to tap her foot in the sand. Then she began to tap on the wood shed.

Tap. Tap. Tap.

"I thought the dog ran off by itself," Kevin said. "No one was holding the leash. It was dragged in the sand."

Tap. Tap. Tap. Tap.

Kevin showed Donna the hook on the leash. "A dog couldn't take this off. Someone must have found the dog and thrown away the leash. But I don't know why."

Tap. Tap. Tap.

Donna turned and looked at the shed. "Maybe it's in here. Maybe the dog is in here." She banged hard on the shed.

"Shh. Quiet," Kevin told her. He put his ear against the shed. "Listen. If a dog is locked in a dark shed, it will whine and scratch on the door."

Donna put her ear against the side of the shed, too. But it was quiet inside the shed.

Donna said, "Maybe someone was sitting here and saw the dog. He took off the leash. Then he stole the dog and left the beach."

"Maybe," Kevin said. "But I don't think so. Why would he take off the leash?"

Donna started to walk away from the shed. "Come on," she told Kevin. "We're not going to find anything here. Let's go back to the sand castle contest."

Kevin walked slowly behind Donna. He was looking down as he walked, and thinking. Kevin didn't notice that Donna had stopped walking. He bumped into her.

"Look over there," Donna whispered. She pointed to a woman sitting under a large orange and yellow umbrella. The woman was facing the water. Kevin couldn't see her face.

"Look at that large bag next to her. It keeps moving," Donna said.

Kevin looked at the large canvas bag. It *was* moving. It seemed that something was inside the bag and wanted to get out.

"We found the dog," Donna said. She started to run toward the woman.

Kevin called to Donna, "Wait." He quickly caught up with her and said, "Don't do anything yet. We're still not sure what's in the bag."

Kevin and Donna walked slowly toward the woman. She was sitting on a large beach chair. The chair's legs had sunk deep into the sand.

"We know what's inside that bag," Donna said when she was facing the woman.

The woman was knitting with two long metal needles. As she moved the needles, she pulled a strand of pink wool from the canvas bag. And as she pulled the wool out, the bag moved.

The woman looked up. She smiled and said, "Excuse me?"

Kevin quickly said, "That's a lovely sweater you're making."

"Thank you, but it's not a sweater. I'm knitting a blanket for a baby."

Arf. Arf.

"Is there just wool in that bag?" Donna asked. "Or do you have a dog in there?"

Arf. Arf.

"Look, look," Kevin said to Donna. He pointed to the ocean. A small white dog was standing at the edge of the water and nibbling at the sand.

Kevin and Donna ran to the dog. It looked up. Then it nibbled the sand some more.

Kevin bent down and petted the dog. Then he tried to attach its leash. He couldn't.

"The dog wasn't stolen," Kevin said. He stood up. "The *collar* was stolen!"

CHAPTER SIX

"There were jewels on that collar, lots of them," Donna said. "Someone took off the leash to get the collar."

The dog began to walk off.

"Don't let it get away," Donna told Kevin, as she followed the dog. "If we return it to Mrs. Rogers, maybe she'll give us a reward. And maybe she'll put our picture in the newspaper."

The dog stopped again to nibble at the sand. It walked ahead and then stopped to nibble again.

"What's in that sand? Why does the dog keep stopping?" Donna asked.

When the dog walked ahead, Kevin felt the sand. It was wet. He picked up the wet sand and smelled it.

"This smells like hamburger. And here's a tiny piece of meat. Someone led that dog away with a trail of hamburger meat. Then when no one was looking, he stole its collar."

Kevin and Donna followed the dog for a while. Then Kevin picked it up and carried it to where Mrs. Rogers had been sitting.

"Now she's gone, too," Donna said.

Kevin and Donna stood on the wooden walkway and looked around. Many of the sand sculptures looked almost finished. They saw a large castle with many towers, a sea monster with two heads, a turtle, a car, and

Gary and Diane's hippo. Then they saw Mrs. Rogers. She was standing in the sand. Her driver was standing nearby and holding her shoes. Kevin and Donna walked toward Mrs. Rogers and heard her calling, "Chester! Chester!"

Mrs. Rogers saw Kevin holding her dog. She ran to them with her arms out. "Oh, Chester, my Chester!" she said.

The dog jumped into her arms. Mrs. Rog-

ers held him tight and kissed him on the nose. Then she looked straight at Chester and said, "Don't you ever run off again. I was so worried."

Arf. Arf.

"Do we get a reward?" Donna asked.

"What?"

"We found your dog at the other end of the beach," Kevin told her. "And we found his leash. But someone stole his collar."

"Ask her about the reward," Donna whispered.

"That collar cost a lot of money," the driver told Kevin. "The diamonds on it were real. How do we know *you* didn't steal it?"

"Oh, you're being foolish," Mrs. Rogers said. "If these nice children stole the collar, they wouldn't have brought Chester back. Please give me my shoes," she said, as she put Chester down.

The driver gave Mrs. Rogers her shoes. She stepped onto the walkway. Then she held onto the driver's shoulder as she wiped the sand from her feet and put on her shoes.

The driver, Kevin, Donna, and Chester followed Mrs. Rogers to her wicker chair.

"Hi," Gary and Diane said, as the group walked past their hippo.

"Your hippo looks great," Donna whispered to them.

The woman in section 13 was busy making a design on the back of her turtle.

Chester looked straight at the turtle. Chester tilted his head to the right and then to the left. But the turtle didn't move.

Arf. Arf. Chester barked at the turtle and then walked away.

The man in the next section was spraying water on the roof of his car made of sand. Then he was patting it smooth. Kevin pointed out the license plate to Donna. It said AUTO 1. Chester sniffed at the tires for a moment.

Arf. Arf. Chester barked again as they walked past the sea monster with two heads.

Mrs. Rogers was sitting in her chair. Chester jumped into her lap.

"You children will get a reward," Mrs. Rogers told Kevin and Donna. "And Fred," she said to her driver, "call the police right away. Tell them the diamond collar was stolen. It must be found."

CHAPTER SEVEN

The driver quickly went along the wooden walkway to the beach entrance.

"The police will be here soon," Mrs. Rogers told Kevin and Donna. "There's a telephone in my car. Fred will call from there."

Mrs. Rogers petted her dog. She hugged him and said, "I've had Chester since he was a puppy. I found him through an ad in the *Morning News*."

Donna said, "*We* found him by following the trail he made when he dragged his leash across the sand."

"Someone led him away by dropping hamburger meat in the sand," Kevin said.

"Excuse me." It was Betty Lane. She was holding her whistle. "I'm just about to end the contest. Then, in a few minutes, we'll announce the winner."

Mrs. Rogers said, "Let's take a quick look at what everyone has made." She took off her shoes again and then walked onto the sand. Kevin and Donna followed her.

They saw the baseball player first. He was lying down in the sand with a bat in his hands. He seemed ready to hit a ball.

They saw a castle with many round towers along the wall. The girl building the castle was carefully scratching lines on the towers and walls to make it look like they were made of brick.

"Do you remember when she first started

building that castle?" Kevin said. "She kept running to the ocean to get water."

Kevin stopped walking. "And I remember the man who was carrying a bucket. He ran past us going that way."

Kevin turned and looked toward the beach entrance. Next to the entrance was the snack stand selling french fries, soda, ice cream, milkshakes, and hamburgers.

Trill. Trill.

Betty Lane blew her whistle. "Everyone please stop working. Robert Wool, Barbara Sands, and I will take one last look. Then we will choose the winner."

The three judges walked from section to section. They smiled and complimented each sand sculpture.

"It was the man from section 12," Donna said to Kevin. "He was the one running toward the snack stand."

"And if he made that hamburger trail, he would have had meat on his hands," Kevin said. "And there might be some meat on his sand sculpture, too."

"Mrs. Rogers, Mrs. Rogers," Donna said, "we know who stole Chester's collar."

Trill. Trill.

The judges were standing near section 6. "It is our pleasure to tell you that this year's winners of the *Morning News* sand castle contest are Jack and Mildred Bradmore. We invite all of you to come and look at their two-headed sea monster."

Many people began walking past Mrs. Rogers, Kevin, and Donna to look at the sea monster.

"Mrs. Rogers! Mrs. Rogers!" her driver called. He was waving his arms as he walked onto the beach. Two police officers were with him.

"You should take the picture soon," Betty Lane told Mrs. Rogers, "before high tide washes away the sea monster."

"That will have to wait," Mrs. Rogers

said. Then she went to talk to the police officers. "Chester's collar was black and there were diamonds on it," she told them.

"We know where it is. We know who stole it," Donna said.

The two police officers, Mrs. Rogers, and the driver turned and looked at Kevin and Donna.

"We found Chester," Kevin told them. "And he was sniffing the sand near one of the sculptures."

"It was the same man who was running to the hamburger stand. He must have had some meat on his hands when he patted the sand on his car," Donna said.

One of the police officers scratched his head and said, "I don't understand what you're telling us."

"I do," Mrs. Rogers said. "Now which man was it? Who stole Chester's collar?"

"It was the man in section 12," Donna said.

CHAPTER EIGHT

They all turned to look at the man in section 12. Mrs. Rogers started to walk toward him.

"Stop. Don't go to him," one of the police officers told her. "We can't search him. To do that, we need a special court order."

"But we can watch him," the other police officer said. "If he stole the dog's collar, he's not going to leave here without it."

The man in section 12 was wearing just

a blue bathing suit. He stood in his section and watched people rush by to look at the sea monster.

The man put his bucket, small shovel, stick, and the paper outline of the car into a straw beach bag. Then he stood very close to the trunk of the car. He looked around. When it seemed that no one was watching, he pushed his hand into the sand and pulled something out.

One of the police officers took a few quick steps over to the man. "May I see that?" he asked.

"What?"

"I want to see what you have in your hand. We're looking for a missing dog collar. That may be it."

The man looked at what he held in his hand. It was a black dog collar with diamonds on it.

"Oh, this," the man said. "I just found it in the trunk of my car."

Arf. Arf.

"That's Chester's collar," Mrs. Rogers said.

The police officer gave her the collar. She put Chester down and was about to put on the collar when Chester ran to the man's beach bag. Chester took out the plastic bucket with his teeth and began licking it.

"There was meat in that bucket. That's why he's licking it," Kevin said.

The two police officers led the man away.

"Come here, Chester. Come here," Mrs. Rogers said.

Gary and Diane were walking away from the sea monster. They saw Kevin and Donna.

"The judges said that our hippo looks real. But we didn't win," Gary told them.

Donna held Diane's hand and told Mrs. Rogers, "This is my sister. We're twins."

"And this is Gary, my twin brother," Kevin said.

"Two sets of twins. That's interesting," Mrs. Rogers said. "Well, you may not have won the contest, but you *will* get your picture in my newspaper."

She turned to her driver and said, "Fred, please get the camera. First we'll take a picture of the Bradmores and their sea monster. Then we'll take a picture of the two sets of twins with Chester and the hippo.

And I'll write an article about them. I will call it 'Brave Twins Catch Thief.' "

"I like that," Kevin said.

"I'll cut out the picture and the article and save them forever," Donna said.

"When did you catch a thief?" Gary asked.

Kevin was about to tell his brother, when Mrs. Rogers stopped him. "He can read all about it tomorrow in the *Morning News*!"